I0748234

FALL OF THE BURROW

Laura Shenton

FALL OF THE BURROW

Laura Shenton

Iridescent Toad Publishing

Iridescent Toad Publishing.

©Laura Shenton 2025
All rights reserved.

Laura Shenton asserts the moral right to be identified as the author of this work.

No part of this publication may be reproduced, stored or transmitted in any form or by any means, electronic, mechanical, photocopying, recording, scanning, or otherwise without written permission from the publisher. It is illegal to copy this book, post it to a website, or distribute it by any other means without permission.

This book is entirely a work of fiction. The names, characters and incidents portrayed in it are the work of the author's imagination. Any resemblance to actual persons, living or dead, events or localities is entirely coincidental.

Designations used by companies to distinguish their products are often claimed as trademarks. All brand names and product names used in this book and on its cover are trade names, service marks, trademarks and registered trademarks of their respective owners. The publishers and the book are not associated with any product or vendor mentioned in this book. None of the companies referenced within the book have endorsed the book.

Cover by Achlys Book Cover Design.

First edition. ISBN 978-1-913779-50-4

Chapter One

Terwilliger crouched in the shadows of the chamber, his dark fur blending seamlessly with the oppressive gloom as he watched another "justice gathering" unfold with grim anticipation. His paw unconsciously traced the jagged scar running across his chest – a permanent, puckered reminder of his own harrowing day before the council. The memory made his breath catch, a momentary tightness in his throat that he quickly suppressed. Around him, the chamber's earthen walls were reinforced with an intricate lattice of salvaged twigs and roots, giving the appearance of a miniature forest turned inward upon itself, as if the outside world had been captured and contorted to serve the burrow's needs. The scent of damp soil and countless rabbit bodies hung heavy in the air, mingling with the acrid undertone of fear.

At the centre of the chamber, flanked by his vigilant loyal guards with their impassive expressions and ready weapons, sat Thornback, the self-proclaimed Sovereign of Woodburrow. What had once been a position of respected leadership, passed down through generations of wise elders, was now nothing more than an elaborate throne for a tyrant who ruled through intimidation rather than wisdom. The large rabbit's fur was sleek and well-groomed, almost lustrous under the sparse light of the root-lanterns, a stark contrast to the matted, dull coats of his subjects. His substantial bulk spoke of regular, plentiful meals while others around him grew increasingly gaunt, their ribs visible beneath thinning fur, their eyes sunken into their skulls.

"Bring forth the accused," Thornback commanded, his voice carrying easily through the hushed chamber, bouncing off the dirt walls and reverberating in Terwilliger's sensitive ears.

Two rabbits – guards chosen for their size and unquestioning loyalty – dragged forward a trembling doe, her whiskers quivering in barely contained terror, ears flattened against her skull in submission. Terwilliger recognised her with a sinking feeling in his stomach – Meadowsweet, a gentle soul known for her healing knowledge and kindness, who had never harmed anyone in the warren. The sight of her reduced to this state made his paws clench involuntarily, claws digging into the soft earth beneath him.

"Meadowsweet of the eastern tunnels," Thornback began, his tone one of rehearsed formality that poorly masked the satisfaction beneath, "you stand accused of hoarding provisions beyond your allocated ration, a serious offence against the collective welfare of Woodburrow. How do you plead?"

The doe's voice was barely audible, a whisper that nonetheless carried in the unnatural silence of the chamber. "I only saved a few seeds for my kits," she explained, her words catching on the edge of a suppressed sob. "They're still growing, their bodies developing, and the rations – they're simply not enough to sustain them. Their fur is falling out in patches. I couldn't bear to watch them suffer when I had the means to help. I only wanted to…"

"The rations," Thornback interrupted, his ears twitching with barely concealed annoyance at her explanation, "are distributed according to status and contribution to our society. Your status does not entitle your offspring to more than what is allocated by my council." He leaned forward on his elevated seat, eyes narrowed to predatory slits, whiskers bristling. "The rule exists for the benefit of all, not the privileged few. I ask you plainly: did you or did you not conceal food against express prohibition?"

A long, excruciating pause stretched through the chamber, during which Terwilliger could hear nothing but the rapid drumming of his own heart and the collective, shallow breathing of the assembled rabbits. Finally, Meadowsweet nodded once, her eyes downcast, defeat evident in every line of her posture.

"The penalty is three days in the pit, followed by reduced rations for a full moon cycle." Thornback's decree brought a collective shudder to the assembled rabbits, a ripple of horror that moved through the crowd like a physical wave. Several mothers pulled their young closer instinctively. The pit was a deep, narrow hole – claustrophobic, perpetually damp and bone-chillingly cold, where prisoners stood in ankle-deep, murky water with no room to sit or lie down, no respite from the constant discomfort and growing exhaustion.

Terwilliger had endured it once, after speaking out against one of Thornback's earlier edicts. The memory of those endless hours – standing in frigid water until his limbs went numb, the darkness so complete it seemed to press against his eyeballs – made his fur stand on end. Some prisoners never returned from it at all, their bodies simply giving out or their minds breaking under the isolation.

As the guards dragged Meadowsweet away, her heartbreaking cries for mercy echoing down the winding tunnels, gradually fading into a haunting silence, Terwilliger slipped from the chamber, his decision crystallising with each step. He'd been methodically planning his escape for weeks, carefully mapping the least-used tunnels in his mind, noting the guard rotations and their patterns, stockpiling what meagre provisions he could safely hide without arousing suspicion.

Tonight would be the night. The image of Meadowsweet's terrified face, the thought of her kits waiting in fear for their mother's return – he could bear no more of this systematic cruelty. His conscience, already weighted with countless witnessed injustices, would fracture entirely if he remained.

Back in his sleeping nook – little more than a shallow depression scraped into the wall of a communal chamber shared with dozens of other rabbits of similarly low status – Terwilliger gathered his few precious possessions with trembling paws. A small pouch fashioned from dried, overlapping leaves carefully sewn together with plant fibres would carry the seeds and dried berries he'd painstakingly saved, one morsel at a time, from his own meagre rations. His dagger, crafted from a shard of flint bound to a broken twig, slid into the crude sheath on his frayed belt. The worn leather coat, salvaged from a past when traders occasionally visited the burrow bringing exotic goods from distant warrens, had become his second skin through years of constant wear. Its multiple pockets, some hidden within the lining, held various essential tools of survival: a length of strong twine that had taken months to accumulate, a small cutting stone honed to razor sharpness, a spark striker made from flint and steel that had belonged to his father – perhaps the only inheritance from a rabbit he barely remembered.

As twilight descended outside, casting the entire burrow into deeper shades of darkness relieved only by the occasional root-lantern with its sickly glow, Terwilliger made his final, meticulous preparations. Movement in the burrow gradually diminished as most rabbits retreated to their sleeping chambers, hoping against hope that a night's rest would somehow make tomorrow's backbreaking labour more bearable. The hours crawled by with excruciating slowness until, finally, the midnight patrol passed his section with their usual cursory glance into the communal sleeping area.

It was time.

With practiced silence born of necessity, Terwilliger navigated the narrow, twisting passages that led towards the seldom-used northern exit, every sense heightened with tension. This particular opening had fallen into dangerous disrepair years ago when Thornback declared it "strategically unnecessary" and reassigned the maintenance crew to expanding his private chambers instead, another example of resources diverted to luxury while infrastructure crumbled. Now, partially collapsed and considered structurally unstable by most, it was guarded by only a single, often drowsy sentry deemed unworthy of more important posts.

Tonight, that sentry was Blackthorn, an older rabbit who had lost part of his left ear in some forgotten confrontation from the time before Thornback's rise to power. Terwilliger had deliberately chosen this night specifically because Blackthorn was well-known to nod off during his watch, particularly after the weekly distribution of fermented berry juice – another luxury Thornback ensured flowed freely to his guards to maintain their loyalty while common rabbits went without.

True to form, Blackthorn sat propped against the earthen wall, his breathing deep and rhythmic, whiskers twitching slightly with each exhalation. His ceremonial spear lay across his lap, its point dulled from neglect, unused and unneeded in this forgotten corner of the warren. Terwilliger crept forward with the silence of a shadow, carefully avoiding the scattered pebbles and twigs that might announce his presence with a telltale crunch or snap.

Just a few more cautious steps, and he would be past the guard's position. Beyond lay the narrow, debris-filled tunnel that would take him to the surface and sweet, long-dreamed-of freedom. The thought made his heart race with a mixture of terror and exhilaration.

"Running away, are we?" The voice – soft, feminine, with an otherworldly echo that seemed to come from everywhere and nowhere at once – coalesced behind him.

Terwilliger spun, dagger instantly in paw, muscles coiled to strike, only to freeze in complete astonishment. Hovering several inches above the ground was a mouse, glowing with a pale blue luminescence that cast eerie, dancing shadows on the tunnel walls and illuminated the sleeping guard's face without waking him. She wore what appeared to be armour of an ancient, unfamiliar design, with intricate engravings that seemed to shift when viewed directly, and in her diminutive paw gleamed a sword that seemed carved from ice or crystal, reflecting light that had no visible source.

Most shocking of all, Terwilliger could see the wall through her translucent form – as if she were made of nothing more substantial than mist.

"W-what are you?" he stammered, keeping his voice to a barely audible whisper to avoid waking Blackthorn, whose continued slumber seemed miraculous in the presence of such an apparition.

The spectral mouse tilted her head, studying him with eyes that held an ageless wisdom and a hint of something that might have been amusement. "My name is Silia. I was once Captain of the Guard in a warren not unlike this one, though that was many seasons ago, before your grandparents' grandparents were born." She gestured with her crystalline sword towards the sleeping guard. "You show good judgment in your timing, Terwilliger. Your planning skills are impressive."

"How do you know my name?" The question escaped his lips before he could consider the wisdom of interrogating a ghost.

"I know many things about you. I've been watching you for some time, longer than you might imagine." Silia floated closer, and Terwilliger suppressed a violent shiver as the temperature around him plummeted, his breath suddenly visible in the chilled air. "I know you're planning to abandon Woodburrow to its fate, to seek your fortune elsewhere while leaving the others to Thornback's mercies."

Shame and defiance warred within him, creating a knot of emotion in his chest. "There's nothing left for me here," he defended, paws clenching and unclenching. "Nothing left for anyone except suffering and slow starvation. One rabbit cannot change what Woodburrow has become."

"Is that so?" Silia circled him slowly, her ethereal form leaving a trail of shimmering particles that dissipated into nothingness.

"Then tell me why you risked severe punishment to share your already insufficient rations with old Whitefoot when he was too ill to work last winter. Or why you taught the younger rabbits to read the old runes when Thornback declared such education unnecessary and potentially seditious."

Terwilliger's ears flattened against his head, his posture becoming defensive. "Small acts. Meaningless gestures against the backdrop of Thornback's institutionalised cruelty. They changed nothing in the end."

"No act of compassion is meaningless," Silia replied, her voice carrying the weight of centuries. "The ripples of kindness spread in ways unseen, even in the darkest of times. You care more than you admit, even to yourself. I've seen your dreams, Terwilliger – they're not of solitary freedom but of a restored Woodburrow."

"Caring hasn't changed anything," Terwilliger growled, a surge of bottled frustration rising within him. "Dreams don't fill empty bellies or heal the wounded. Now move aside, spirit. Don't make me regret speaking with you. I've made my decision after much deliberation."

"Have you?" Silia's voice hardened, the temperature dropping further until frost began to form on the tunnel walls. "Then you've decided that Meadowsweet and her innocent kits deserve their fate without anyone to speak for them. You've decided that Whitefoot should die alone in the darkness after all he's contributed to this warren. You've decided that the younglings who look up to you, who whisper your name with hope, should grow up believing that when things become difficult, the answer is to run rather than to stand and fight for what's right."

Each word struck like a physical blow, landing with precision on the doubts Terwilliger had been desperately trying to suppress. His grip tightened on his dagger until his knuckles ached, the blade trembling slightly in his grasp.

"What would you have me do?" he demanded, desperation leaking into his voice despite his efforts to contain it. "I'm one rabbit against Thornback and all his guards. One voice that's easily silenced, one life that would be snuffed out at the first sign of rebellion."

"One rabbit can be enough," Silia said, her glow intensifying until Terwilliger had to squint against its brilliance. "Especially one with courage, intelligence, a strong moral compass, and..." she nodded towards the sleeping guard, "...the capacity for careful planning. History pivots on the actions of individuals who refuse to accept what others call inevitable."

"You're suggesting I overthrow Thornback?" Terwilliger couldn't keep the disbelief from his voice, the idea so audacious it bordered on absurdity. "That's madness. It's suicide, plain and simple."

"Is it?" Silia's smile held secrets accumulated across countless seasons. "I've seen burrows rise and fall throughout the centuries, Terwilliger. I've witnessed the mightiest armies defeated by the smallest obstacles. I've seen tyrants toppled by those they least suspected – the servants they ignored, the subjects they dismissed. And I've been waiting, watching through long years for someone like you – someone who hasn't yet lost the ability to hope for something better despite overwhelming evidence to the contrary."

Behind them, Blackthorn snorted in his sleep and shifted position, one paw twitching as if chasing something in a dream. Terwilliger tensed, muscles coiled to flee at the slightest indication the guard might wake, but the older rabbit merely settled back into his slumber with a contented sigh.

Silia floated closer, her spectral face inches from Terwilliger's, her eyes containing galaxies of experiences he could barely comprehend. "Go if you must. I cannot and will not physically stop you. But know this: beyond these walls lies not the freedom you imagine, but wilderness filled with predators who hunt rabbits for sport and hardships that will test you far more severely than Thornback ever could. The owl's silent wings, the fox's cunning, the weasel's relentless pursuit – these await the solitary rabbit. At least here, you fight for something greater than mere survival. You fight for the soul of a community that once thrived and could again."

Terwilliger stood motionless, trapped between the sleeping guard and the ghostly mouse, between the promise of escape and the weight of responsibility. The truth of her words settled upon him like a physical burden, bowing his shoulders and making his carefully planned escape suddenly seem like the coward's path.

"I can help you," Silia continued, her voice softening to a spectral whisper. "I've witnessed countless rebellions, successful and failed alike. I know strategies and tactics Thornback couldn't begin to imagine. The wisdom of centuries could be at your disposal."

"Why me?" Terwilliger finally asked, the question that had been building since her appearance. "Out of all the rabbits in Woodburrow, why approach me? Why now, when I'm finally prepared to leave?"

"Because despite everything you've witnessed, everything you've endured, you haven't surrendered your soul to fear or despair, unlike so many others who walk these tunnels as mere shells of themselves. You still burn with an inner fire that circumstances haven't extinguished," Silia urged. "You've come right up to the line – ready to leave it all behind – and somehow, you're still here, talking to me. That means something."

The distant sound of approaching footsteps echoed down the tunnel – the next patrol making its rounds earlier than expected, perhaps due to some change in schedule Terwilliger hadn't anticipated. He had mere seconds to decide his fate and potentially that of the entire burrow.

With a last, lingering glance at the exit and the tantalising promise of freedom it represented – freedom from oppression, from responsibility, from the crushing weight of witnessing daily injustice – he turned back towards the heart of the burrow, Silia floating silently beside him.

"I hope I don't regret this," he muttered, his voice barely audible even to his own sensitive ears.

"You will," Silia replied with surprising candour, a ghost of a smile playing across her translucent features. "Many times, in dark moments when the task seems impossible. But you would regret leaving far more, watching from a distance as everything you secretly love crumbles to dust, knowing you might have made a difference had you found the courage to stay."

Chapter Two

Dawn found Terwilliger in the Gathering Roots, the massive central chamber where work assignments were distributed each morning. Golden shafts of early sunlight filtered through narrow air shafts, illuminating dancing motes of dust and casting dappled patterns across the packed earth floor. The space was designed to accommodate hundreds of rabbits, its vaulted ceiling supported by the living roots of the great oak that grew above Woodburrow. These ancient, gnarled roots – thicker than three rabbits standing side by side – twisted and curved overhead like the ribs of some enormous beast. Once, these sessions had been brief and organised, filled with the gentle murmur of conversation and communal planning. Now, they had become another opportunity for Thornback to display his power, the once-comforting ritual transformed into a daily reminder of their subjugation.

As Terwilliger took his place among the workers of his section, nestled between the familiar bodies of rabbits he'd known since kithood, he felt a sudden chill beside him – Silia, invisible to all but him, had kept her word to remain by his side. The ghostly presence made his fur stand slightly on end, though none around him could perceive the cause of his discomfort.

"Remember," her voice whispered in his ear, as clear as if she were corporeal yet audible only to him, "observe today. Look for the discontented, the brave, those who haven't completely surrendered their will. Watch for the subtle signs – a defiant glance, a reluctant bow, a muttered comment quickly silenced. Your first task is to find allies."

The gradual hush that fell over the chamber announced Thornback's approach before he appeared. The large rabbit's customary entourage of guards – burly, scarred fighters with cold eyes and twitching noses – surrounded him as he took his position on the raised platform of compacted earth at the chamber's centre. Thornback moved with the deliberate slowness of one who knew everyone waited on his pleasure, his silver-tipped black fur gleaming with health that stood in stark contrast to the dull coats of many present.

"Today marks the beginning of harvest preparations," Thornback announced, his voice carrying effortlessly through the now-silent space. "The changing seasons wait for no rabbit, and neither will our efforts. Output quotas will increase by one-third effective immediately. Any section failing to meet their quota will see their rations reduced accordingly." His tone suggested this was a reasonable request rather than the potential death sentence many recognised it to be.

A ripple of dismay passed through the assembled rabbits – the subtle flattening of ears, widening of eyes, and tightening of whiskers that conveyed their distress without making a sound. With resources already stretched thin and many tunnels receiving less than half the food they had under previous leadership, many were barely surviving on current rations. Mothers exchanged worried glances, thinking of kits already going to sleep hungry.

"Furthermore," Thornback continued, seemingly oblivious to the distress his words caused, his paw tapping impatiently against the earthen dais, "I have received reports of seditious talk in the lower tunnels. Whispers in corners, complaints in the darkness. Let me remind you that criticism of leadership is treason against the burrow itself." His gaze swept the crowd, lingering deliberately on certain sections where trouble had previously emerged. "The punishment for treason remains death. Swift, public, and without exception."

Terwilliger felt fear clutch at his heart, that familiar constriction that had become almost a constant companion these past seasons. But alongside it rose something unexpected – anger, burning hotter and brighter than he'd allowed himself to feel before. The injustice of it all – the starvation amid plenty, the fear replacing community, the slow death of everything that had once made Woodburrow worth defending – crystallised into a molten core within him.

He glanced around the chamber, studying the faces of his fellow rabbits with new awareness. Most showed the blank resignation he'd come to expect, the carefully neutral expressions that had become their best defence. But here and there, he caught glimpses of the same anger he felt – quickly masked, but unmistakable in the tightening of a jaw, the narrowing of eyes, the subtle tension in shoulders prepared to act rather than merely endure.

"There," Silia murmured, indicating a sturdy female near the chamber's eastern entrance. Her brown fur was streaked with grey at the muzzle, and a notch in her left ear spoke of old battles survived. "Briarwood. Former tunneller before she spoke against Thornback's expansion plans. Said the new tunnels would weaken the burrow's defences rather than strengthen them. She hasn't broken. Watch how the others unconsciously position themselves around her – they still look to her for guidance, though none would admit it."

Terwilliger gave an imperceptible nod, careful not to appear to be responding to an unseen presence. He knew Briarwood by reputation – strong, clever, and blunt to the point of recklessness. She had designed irrigation systems that still served the community gardens, despite Thornback's attempts to claim credit for their success.

"And the old one near the back," Silia continued, directing Terwilliger's attention to a frail-looking rabbit with exceptionally pale fur who stood slightly apart from the others. "Sage. He remembers the burrow before Thornback, before Thornback's predecessor even. The youngsters respect him, though he rarely speaks these days. His silence is deliberate – he knows Thornback would eliminate him if he recognised the influence he still holds. Look at how the younger ones position themselves protectively around him."

As work assignments were distributed by Thornback's lieutenants – a process deliberately made humiliating through random rejections and reassignments – Terwilliger memorised the names and faces Silia pointed out. Each potential ally had their own story, their own grievance, their own small acts of defiance hidden beneath a veneer of compliance. By the time he received his own assignment – root gathering in the western forest section, a task both arduous and dangerous – he had identified several potential allies scattered throughout Woodburrow's social hierarchy.

"Not enough for an open confrontation," Silia cautioned as they made their way towards the western exit, joining the stream of rabbits dispersing to their daily labours. "But enough to begin. Remember, revolutions don't require everyone's participation – just enough to create momentum that others will follow."

The western forest team consisted of twelve rabbits responsible for locating and harvesting edible roots beyond the burrow's immediate vicinity. They carried simple digging implements – sharpened sticks and flattened stones – and woven reed baskets to transport their findings. It was dangerous work – exposing them to hawks, foxes, and other predators that considered rabbit a delicacy – but it offered something rare and increasingly precious in Woodburrow: relative freedom from constant supervision.

Among the team was Tansy, a quiet doe with sharp amber eyes and dexterous paws whom

Silia had identified as trustworthy. Unlike many who laboured under Thornback's rule, her movements remained quick and precise, wasting no energy but accomplishing more than those around her. As they worked their way through the underbrush, carefully digging around promising plants and assessing which roots could be harvested without killing valuable growth, Terwilliger manoeuvred to position himself near her.

"Heavy quotas this moon," he remarked casually, his voice pitched just loud enough to reach her ears while checking to ensure none of Thornback's known informants were within earshot. His paws continued their work, maintaining the appearance of ordinary conversation between labourers.

Tansy glanced at him, wariness evident in her expression, her whiskers twitching slightly as she evaluated his intentions. "No heavier than we've borne before," she replied neutrally, her tone revealing nothing of her true thoughts as she efficiently extracted a tangle of wild carrots from the loamy soil.

"True. Though I wonder how much heavier they'll become before we can bear no more."

Terwilliger kept his voice conversational, but allowed just enough genuine emotion to colour his words, a calculated risk to suggest his discontent was real rather than a trap to expose hers.

Her paws stilled in the soil, just for a moment, the briefest hesitation that spoke volumes. "Dangerous thoughts, Terwilliger." The warning was clear, but not delivered with the automatic fear that marked true believers in Thornback's regime.

"Dangerous times," he countered softly, meeting her gaze directly for the first time, allowing her to see something of the resolve that had taken root within him since his encounter with Silia.

She studied him for a long moment before returning to her digging, her movements methodical and precise. "My brother died in the pit last season," she said, referring to the notorious punishment chamber. "Starvation, they said, though he'd only been there four days." Her voice remained conversational, as if discussing the weather, but her eyes held a smouldering fury that no amount of careful control could entirely conceal. "Officially, he was hoarding food. In truth, he questioned why the guards needed new quarters while families were crowded into crumbling tunnels."

"I'm sorry," Terwilliger said, and meant it, understanding that her loss was just one among countless tragedies unfolding beneath Thornback's rule.

"Save your sorrow." Tansy extracted a thick root with a particularly forceful motion and placed it in her collection basket, the thud of it landing heavier than necessary. "What I want to know is why you're suddenly asking questions that could land you in the same pit. You've never been one for politics, Terwilliger. You keep to yourself, do your work, survive. Why risk that now?"

Silia floated to Terwilliger's side, her form ever-translucent in the dappled forest light. "Tell her the truth," the ghost advised, her expression intent. "Not about me – but about your intentions. She needs to know this isn't a trap."

"Because I almost left last night," he admitted, meeting Tansy's gaze. "I stood at the northern exit, ready to leave all of this behind. Ready to take my chances alone in the wild rather than keep living under Thornback's paw." He swallowed hard, the memory of his near-desertion still sharp. "But then I realised I couldn't live with myself if I did. Running would solve nothing, change nothing – it would only leave everyone else to suffer while I saved myself."

Tansy's expression revealed nothing, her features schooled into the careful blankness that had become second nature to those surviving under tyranny, but her next words came in a whisper so faint he had to lean closer to hear. "There are others who feel as you do. Not many, but enough. We meet in the abandoned storage tunnels beneath the eastern quadrant when the moon is dark. Three nights from now." With that, she moved away, leaving Terwilliger to process this unexpected development as she resumed harvesting several paces distant, as if their conversation had never happened.

"Well done," Silia said, approval evident in her tone as she hovered beside him. "It seems the seeds of rebellion were already planted.

You need only help them grow. Now be careful – he's watching."

Terwilliger followed her gaze to spot Nettle, one of the younger workers known to curry favour with the guards. Recognising he was being observed with poorly disguised interest, Terwilliger lowered his head and returned to his digging with renewed vigour, giving no indication that anything significant had transpired.

Chapter Three

The remainder of the day passed in exhausting labour, the heat of the sun intensifying as it climbed towards its zenith, then gradually relenting as afternoon shadows lengthened across the forest floor. By sunset, the team had gathered nearly their quota of roots, which would be processed into food, medicine, and emergency rations. As they returned to the burrow, their baskets heavy with their harvest, Terwilliger found himself studying his surroundings with new eyes.

The great oak above Woodburrow spread its branches protectively over the main entrances, its massive trunk scarred by seasons of weather and wildlife, yet standing strong. Its roots formed natural support structures throughout the upper tunnels, living architecture that had served generations of rabbits. The surrounding forest provided resources and hiding places in equal measure, with countless escape routes known only to those who regularly worked above ground. What had once seemed a prison might, with the right perspective, be recognised as a fortress – defensible, sustainable, and ripe for reclamation.

That night, in the privacy of his sleeping nook, Terwilliger conferred with Silia. The sounds of the burrow settling for the night – kits being soothed to sleep, the soft snoring of elderly rabbits, and the gentle rustle of bedding as others settled in – masked his clandestine conversation.

"If there's already an organised resistance, why haven't they acted?" he asked, keeping his voice to a bare whisper while pretending to arrange his bedding, should anyone pass by his modest dwelling. "Why suffer season after season under Thornback if they have the numbers to challenge him?"

Silia's ghostly form paced the small space, her tail swishing in agitation, passing occasionally through the solid earth of the walls as if they were mere illusion.

"Resistance isn't the same as rebellion," she explained, her voice tinged with the wisdom of one who had seen many conflicts. "They may share grievances, perhaps even fantasise about change, but taking action requires leadership. Vision." She paused, fixing him with her penetrating gaze that seemed to evaluate not just who he was, but who he could become. "It requires someone willing to risk everything when success is merely possible, not certain."

"And you think that's me?" Terwilliger couldn't keep the doubt from his voice as he smoothed a particularly stubborn tuft of bedding grass. "I'm no leader, Silia. I've spent my life avoiding attention, not seeking it."

"I know it's you." Silia's certainty was unnerving, her faith in him seemingly unshakable despite his own misgivings. "Sometimes the greatest leaders are those who never sought power – who take it reluctantly, only because they must." Her form shimmered slightly in the darkness. "But first, you need information. Thornback's weaknesses, the guard rotations, the location of food stores. Before you meet with Tansy's group, gather whatever intelligence you can. Knowledge is your first weapon."

The next two days passed in a blur of careful observation and discreet conversations. Terwilliger used his reputation as a solitary, harmless oddity to move through the burrow's various sections, noting guard patterns and structural vulnerabilities. He volunteered for additional water-carrying duties, which granted him access to areas normally restricted, and offered to assist elderly rabbits whose gratitude loosened their tongues about the burrow's history and hidden passages.

He learnt the details of how the guards' loyalty was maintained through extra rations and privileges: private sleeping quarters, first selection of mates, immunity from work rotations – but that several among them harboured doubts about Thornback's increasingly erratic commands. Their obedience stemmed more from fear of their fellow guards than genuine devotion to their leader. He discovered that the main food storage chambers were less guarded during the changing of shifts, a brief window of vulnerability that occurred three times daily.

Most valuably, he confirmed what he'd long suspected – Thornback never ate or drank anything that hadn't been tested by one of his servants, suggesting a deep-seated fear of poisoning that contradicted his air of invulnerability.

On the third night, as the burrow settled into its nocturnal rhythm, Terwilliger made his way towards the eastern quadrant. The abandoned storage tunnels were accessible only through a narrow passage behind one of the community sleeping chambers, a forgotten remnant of the burrow's original design. Navigating through the darkness, using his whiskers and paw pads to sense the walls in the absence of light, he felt rather than saw Silia's presence beside him, her ghostly glow providing comfort but no practical illumination.

"Be honest but cautious," she advised as they neared their destination, the tunnel gradually widening as they descended. "These rabbits have survived by trusting no one. They'll be testing you as much as you're evaluating them. Remember: hope is dangerous to those who have learnt to live without it. Don't promise what you can't deliver."

The tunnel opened into a small chamber where the remains of old storage structures – woven reed shelves now sagging with age and disuse – created convenient seating. Oil lamps burned low, their flames carefully shielded to prevent light from escaping into the main tunnels, casting long shadows across the assembled rabbits – twelve in all, including Tansy, Briarwood, and old Sage.

Briarwood, her powerful form tensed as if ready for conflict, her notched ear twitching with barely contained energy, spoke first. "You've taken a significant risk coming here, Terwilliger. Why?" Her directness cut through any pretence of casual meeting, demanding immediate truth.

All eyes turned to him, suspicious, evaluating, desperate in equal measure, and in that moment, Terwilliger realised that his answer would either open a door or seal his fate. Drawing himself to his full height, conscious of Silia's presence behind him, he spoke the truth that had crystallised within him over the past few days.

"Because Woodburrow doesn't belong to Thornback. It belongs to all of us – to our ancestors who dug these tunnels, to the kits who deserve a future better than fear and hunger." His voice strengthened as he continued, surprising even himself with its clarity and conviction. "I'm here because I believe we can reclaim it. Not just survive, but rebuild what's been lost – a community where strength protects rather than oppresses, where resources are shared rather than hoarded. I'm here because I'm tired of watching us forget who we are."

The silence that followed seemed to stretch into infinity, filled only with the soft crackling of the oil lamps.

Then Sage, his fur silvered with age and eyes cloudy but still sharp with intelligence, nodded slowly. "Perhaps," the elder rabbit said, his voice cracking slightly from disuse but carrying the weight of generations, "it's finally time for the old stories to become new history."

Chapter Four

A fortnight had passed since Terwilliger's initiation into the resistance. What had begun as twelve discontented rabbits had carefully expanded to twenty, then thirty. Each new member brought skills and information vital to their growing plan. Some came with knowledge of forgotten pathways, others with connections throughout the warren, and a few with the physical strength needed for what might lie ahead. Sage, despite his advanced seasons, proved to have an encyclopaedic knowledge of the burrow's older tunnels – passages forgotten or sealed under Thornback's rule, but potentially navigable with the right effort. His weathered paws would trace temporary maps in the dirt as he described chambers that hadn't seen a living soul in generations.

Briarwood organised the strongest among them into what she stubbornly refused to call a fighting force. "We're not soldiers," she had insisted during one tense planning session, her dark eyes flashing with passionate conviction. "We're defenders. There's a difference." The distinction mattered to her – they weren't seeking to conquer but to reclaim what had been taken from them all.

Tansy, with her network of connections throughout the warren, became their eyes and ears, bringing reports of Thornback's increasingly paranoid edicts. The latest required all families to surrender one member to serve in the expanded guard – a transparent attempt to place hostages against potential rebellion. Families whispered their fears in the darkness of their chambers, torn between compliance and resistance, while Thornback's lieutenants made examples of those who hesitated.

Tonight, the core group had gathered in their underground meeting place to finalise the first phase of their plan. The chamber was lit by a handful of carefully placed lamps, casting long shadows across the walls. Terwilliger spread out a rough map of the burrow on the earthen floor, portions of it filled in with details provided by various resistance members. His paws moved deftly across the charcoal markings, indicating primary tunnels and vulnerable access points.

"The guard rotation changes at midnight," he explained, pointing to several locations where small X marks indicated posted sentries. "That gives us a brief window to access the primary food storage chamber here. If we can redistribute even a portion of the supplies to the outer chambers, it would provide immediate relief to the most vulnerable families." The outer chambers, where the poorest and most marginalised rabbits dwelled, had suffered the most under Thornback's selective rationing.

"And demonstrate that Thornback isn't as all-powerful as he claims," added Reed, a former guard who had joined their cause after witnessing one too many arbitrary punishments. His intimate knowledge of guard protocols had already proven invaluable. Reed's left ear bore a notch from when he'd intervened in one particularly brutal enforcement action – a visible reminder of the price of compassion in Thornback's regime.

Silia, visible only to Terwilliger, circled the map with a critical eye. Her translucent form passed through the gathered rabbits, who shivered unknowingly as her spectral presence brushed against their fur. "Remind them of the risks," she cautioned, her ethereal voice filled with centuries of witnessed rebellion. "False hope is more dangerous than no hope at all."

Terwilliger nodded slightly, acknowledging her advice while trying not to draw attention to his one-sided communication. "The dangers are significant," he continued aloud, his voice dropping to ensure it wouldn't carry beyond their circle. "If we're discovered, Thornback won't hesitate to make examples of those caught. His retribution will be swift and public. Anyone who wishes to withdraw from this operation should do so now, without shame." He paused, giving weight to the moment, allowing each rabbit present to consider the potential consequences of their actions.

No one moved. The determination in the

faces surrounding him brought a lump to Terwilliger's throat. Each had their own reasons for being there – personal injustices, lost loved ones, or simply the growing frustration of oppression – yet they were united in purpose.

"Then we proceed tonight," he declared, drawing a steadying breath. "Briarwood, your team will create a distraction near the western tunnels. Nothing overtly rebellious – perhaps a minor tunnel collapse that requires immediate attention. Just enough to draw the guards away from our real objective."

Briarwood nodded, her eyes already calculating the perfect location and amount of structural damage needed.

"Reed," Terwilliger continued, "once the guards are drawn away, your group will access the storage chamber. Take only what can be carried inconspicuously. We don't need to empty the stores – just enough to make a difference to those who need it most. Tansy's network will handle distribution over the next few days, ensuring supplies reach those most in need without drawing attention."

As the meeting dispersed, with members leaving individually to avoid notice, Terwilliger remained behind with Sage. The elderly rabbit had been quiet throughout the planning, his whiskers drooping with unspoken concern. The lamps dimmed as the last of the conspirators departed, leaving the chamber in semi-darkness.

"You have doubts," Terwilliger observed once they were alone – or as alone as he ever was with Silia hovering nearby, her spectral form casting faint blue shadows that Sage couldn't perceive.

Sage sighed. "Not doubts. Memories. I've seen resistance before, Terwilliger. Thornback didn't gain power overnight. There were others who stood against him in the beginning, when his intentions first revealed themselves beneath the veneer of leadership."

"What happened to them?" Terwilliger leaned forward, sensing a history that hadn't been shared with the younger members of their group.

The old rabbit's eyes clouded with pain,

memories visibly rippling across his features. "Some disappeared. Taken in the night, never to return. Others were publicly executed, made into spectacles of warning. Many simply... conformed, eventually. Fear is a powerful motivator – especially fear for one's loved ones." His paw unconsciously moved to a faded scar that ran across his chest, visible only when his fur parted just so.

"You think we'll fail?" Terwilliger couldn't keep the edge from his voice, a defensive sharpness born of his own unacknowledged fears.

"I think," Sage replied carefully, his words measured and deliberate, "that success requires more than righteous anger. It requires a vision of what comes after. Thornback rose to power because the previous leadership had grown complacent, corrupt in more subtle ways. If we remove him only to create another form of tyranny, we've accomplished nothing." He looked directly into Terwilliger's eyes. "Destroying is easier than building, young one."

The wisdom in these words resonated deeply. Terwilliger had been so focused on opposition that he'd given little thought to governance afterwards. The silence between them stretched as he contemplated the elder's warning.

"What would you suggest?" he asked, genuinely curious, his earlier defensiveness melting into respect for the old rabbit's experience.

"A council, perhaps. Representatives from each section of the burrow, making decisions collectively. Limits on power, regular rotation of leadership." Sage's eyes took on a distant look, as though peering into the distant past. "It was how things were done in the oldest days, according to the stories my grandmother told. Before the times of scarcity that made some believe that only the strong could ensure survival."

"A worthy goal," Silia commented, her spectral form settling beside the elder rabbit, though he remained unaware of her presence. "Remind him that winning freedom is only the first battle. Maintaining it is the true war."

Terwilliger nodded thoughtfully, echoing her

sentiment. "If we succeed – when we succeed – I hope you'll help establish such a system, Sage. Your wisdom will be essential." He placed a paw briefly on the elder's shoulder. "We'll need those who remember the old ways to guide us towards something better."

The old rabbit's whiskers twitched in what might have been amusement, creasing his face into a web of fine lines. "Let's survive tonight first. Dreams of governance can wait until morning – assuming we see it."

Hours later, as the burrow's main chambers fell into the deep quiet of midnight, Terwilliger found himself positioned at a junction of tunnels that offered a clear view of both the storage chamber entrance and the western passage where Briarwood's team would create their diversion. The night was unnaturally still, the usual ambient sounds of the warren all seemed muted, as though the burrow itself held its breath in anticipation. Silia floated anxiously at his side, her ethereal form undulating with tension.

"Something feels wrong," she murmured as she drifted back and forth in agitation. "The guard pattern is different tonight. There's purpose in their positioning."

Terwilliger had noticed it too. Instead of the usual two guards at the storage entrance, there were four, and they seemed unusually alert. Their ears swivelled at the slightest sound, and they carried their weapons at the ready rather than slung across their backs. Where there should have been bored vigilance, there was anticipation.

"We should abort," he whispered, the words barely audible even to himself. His heart pounded against his ribs, instinct warning him of danger even as his mind sought rational explanations.

But before he could signal to the others, a distinctive rumble echoed from the western tunnels, followed by shouts and the sound of running paws. Briarwood's diversion was underway, the sound of collapsing earth reverberating through the passages. Too late to stop the plan now – events were already in motion.

To Terwilliger's dismay, only two of the storage guards ran towards the commotion.

The remaining two drew their weapons – sharpened sticks reinforced with flint tips – and took up defensive positions, their backs to the storage entrance, eyes scanning the shadows with practiced precision.

From his hiding place, Terwilliger could see Reed and his team approaching from the opposite tunnel, unaware of the changed circumstances. They moved with the silent efficiency they had practiced for days, staying close to the walls where the shadows were deepest. They were moments from exposing themselves to the armed guards, walking into what increasingly felt like a trap.

"I have to warn them," Terwilliger hissed.

"You'll be seen," Silia cautioned, her spectral form flickering with alarm. "They'll capture you."

"Better one than all of us."

Decision made, Terwilliger darted into the open, deliberately making enough noise to draw attention away from the approaching team. His paws struck the earth with uncharacteristic heaviness, scattering pebbles that clattered loudly in the tense silence.

The guards spun towards him, weapons raised. "Halt!" one shouted, the command echoing down the tunnel, his voice carrying the confidence of authority long exercised.

Terwilliger froze, paws raised in apparent surrender. From the corner of his eye, he saw Reed's team register the danger and retreat silently into the shadows, melting back the way they had come. Relief flooded through him, temporarily overwhelming his fear. They had escaped detection – the plan could be salvaged another day.

"Well, what have we here?" The larger guard approached, the tip of his spear gleaming in the dim light as he prodded Terwilliger with it. The sharp point dimpled the fur at Terwilliger's chest. "Out for a midnight stroll, are we?" The guard's tone carried a smug satisfaction that sent a chill through Terwilliger's body.

"I couldn't sleep," Terwilliger replied, injecting a tremor into his voice that wasn't entirely feigned. A prickling heat settled between his shoulder blades, despite the underground chill – a sure sign of nerves he couldn't shake. "I thought a walk might help. The eastern tunnels were too crowded."

"In a restricted area?" The guard's tone made it clear he wasn't fooled, his eyes narrowing with suspicion and something darker – anticipation, perhaps. "Search him."

The second guard roughly patted down Terwilliger's clothing, his paws practiced and thorough, discovering and confiscating his dagger with a grunt of satisfaction. The blade disappeared into the guard's belt. "Armed too. Suspicious behaviour, wouldn't you say, Flint?" His whiskers twitched with barely contained excitement.

The first guard, evidently called Flint, nodded grimly, his scarred muzzle twisting into what might have been a smile on a face less hardened by violence. "Very suspicious. I think the Sovereign will want to speak with this one personally. Perhaps you'll explain to him why you're wandering about with a blade near our food stores."

Terwilliger's heart sank as his paws were bound behind him with coarse twine, pulled tight enough to cut into his skin. The guards made no attempt to be gentle, wrenching his arms back until his shoulders strained painfully. The plan had failed before it even began, and now he faced Thornback's judgment alone.

As the guards marched him towards Thornback's chambers, shoving him forward whenever his pace slowed, Silia kept pace beside him, her expression grim in the darkness of the tunnels.

"This is my fault," she whispered, her voice heavy with self-recrimination. "I should have sensed the trap. Something changed in the patterns – I missed it." Her spectral form wavered with emotion.

"Not your fault," Terwilliger muttered under his breath, keeping his voice low to avoid further punishment from his captors. "Something must have leaked. Someone talked."

The guards shoved him roughly, the butt of a spear striking between his shoulder blades. "Quiet! Who are you talking to?" The larger guard leaned closer, his breath hot against

Terwilliger's ear. "Already cracking, are you? Save the madness for later – you'll need it."

Terwilliger bit back a response, focusing instead on memorising the route and noting the number of guards they passed. If – when – he got another chance, this information would be valuable. They would not catch him again. The pain in his bound paws faded into the background as he concentrated – three guards at this junction, reinforced door there, weakness in the ceiling structure here.

Thornback's private chambers occupied what had once been a communal great hall, according to Sage's histories. Now it was divided into specialised areas – sleeping quarters, a private dining area, and an audience chamber in which official business could be conducted. Once these spaces had hosted celebrations and councils for all rabbits; now they served the comfort of one. Terwilliger was forced to his knees before a raised platform where Thornback reclined on a bed of rare dried grasses, the sweet scent incongruous with the tension in the air.

"Leave us," Thornback commanded the guards after they reported the circumstances of Terwilliger's capture. His voice was surprisingly melodious for one so feared – pleasant, almost, were it not for the undercurrent of controlled malice. The larger rabbit waited until they had withdrawn before sitting up, his cold eyes fixed on his prisoner.

"Terwilliger," he said, the name rolling off his tongue with false cordiality that made it sound like a shared secret. "How disappointing that we should meet in such unfortunate circumstances." He adjusted his position, the dried grasses rustling beneath his considerable weight.

Terwilliger maintained a stony silence, conscious of Silia hovering protectively near his shoulder. Her spectral glow cast no reflection in Thornback's calculating eyes.

"Nothing to say?" Thornback raised an eyebrow, the gesture oddly delicate for his brutal reputation. "Perhaps you'll be more talkative after some time in the pit. The discomfort has a way of loosening tongues, I find. Unless, of course, you'd prefer to tell me who else was involved in tonight's little adventure." He leaned forward, his bulk casting a shadow over Terwilliger. "A collapsed tunnel so conveniently timed near my guard post? Hardly the work of one disgruntled rabbit."

"I was alone," Terwilliger stated flatly, meeting Thornback's gaze with a steadiness he didn't entirely feel. The twine cut deeper into his wrists as he subtly tested its strength.

Thornback chuckled, the sound devoid of warmth, echoing hollowly in the chamber. "Come now. You may be foolish, but you're not stupid. The distraction in the western tunnels was co-ordinated. You had accomplices. Give me names, and perhaps I'll be lenient."

"He's going to torture you," Silia warned, her voice tight with concern as she circled Thornback, studying him with ancient eyes. "And he won't stop until he gets what he wants. He enjoys the process too much."

Terwilliger knew she was right. His options were narrowing rapidly. He could feel the pressure building, the moment of decision upon him. Every heartbeat seemed to echo in the oppressive silence of the chamber.

"If I tell you what you want to know," he said, carefully considering each word, "what guarantee do I have that you'll keep your word about leniency?" A desperate gambit, but he needed time to think, to plan.

Thornback's whiskers twitched in amusement, as though Terwilliger had told an unexpectedly good joke. "None whatsoever. But suffering before death seems rather pointless, doesn't it?" His casual cruelty was all the more chilling for its honesty. "And make no mistake, Terwilliger – death awaits at the end of this path you've chosen. The only variables are how long it takes and how painful it becomes."

In that moment, Terwilliger made his decision. Meeting Thornback's gaze steadily, he spoke with a confidence he didn't entirely feel but was determined to project. "You're going to fall, Thornback. If not by my paw, then by another's. This burrow remembers what it was like before your tyranny, and that memory is more powerful than your fear." The words felt right as they left his mouth, a truth he hadn't fully realised until speaking it aloud.

Thornback's expression hardened, the façade of amiability dropping away to reveal the cold calculation beneath. "Brave words for someone who's about to spend a very long, very painful night in the questioning chamber." He raised his voice in sharp command. "Guards!"

The door opened immediately, revealing that the guards had been listening, awaiting the inevitable summons. Thornback gestured dismissively, as though Terwilliger were merely an unsatisfactory meal to be removed from his sight. "Take him below. Use whatever methods necessary to extract the names of his co-conspirators. Be thorough, but keep him alive – for now."

As the guards seized him, pulling him roughly to his feet, Terwilliger locked eyes with Silia. "Whatever happens," he whispered, his voice barely audible even to himself, "continue the plan. Find another to lead if I can't. Promise me."

64

Chapter Five

The questioning chamber lived up to its euphemistic name. Located deep beneath even the lowest residential tunnels, it was a place few entered and fewer left. Its walls were lined with implements designed for a single purpose: pain – curved hooks, barbed vines, and tools whose function Terwilliger could only guess at in the dim, smoky light cast by torches that seemed to illuminate everything except hope.

Terwilliger lost track of time as Thornback's interrogators applied their trade with methodical precision. They were careful not to inflict mortal damage – a dead prisoner couldn't provide information – but within that constraint, they were thorough. Questions came between each new torment, always the same: names, meeting places, plans. Terwilliger's world narrowed to the rhythm of pain and respite, both designed to break his will.

Through it all, Silia remained by his side, her ghostly presence offering cold comfort when all other comfort was denied. When his resolve wavered, she would whisper stories of other captives who had endured, other tyrants who had fallen. Tales of resistance from ages long past, when her own physical form still walked the earth. When consciousness threatened to slip away, she sang ancient battle songs in a voice only he could hear, keeping him anchored to the waking world when oblivion beckoned seductively.

"They're growing frustrated," she observed during a brief respite when the interrogators stepped out to confer, their hushed voices carrying faintly through the heavy door. Terwilliger hung from restraints that kept him upright when his legs had long since refused to support him. "You've given them nothing useful. Their techniques are failing, and they know Thornback will not accept failure."

Terwilliger, his body a canvas of pain,

managed a broken smile that cracked his dry, split lips. "Small... victories." The words came at great cost, his throat raw from screaming despite his determination to remain silent. He had lost that battle early, but had won the more important one – he had revealed nothing of value, nothing that would endanger his companions.

Dawn was breaking above the burrow when the interrogators finally admitted defeat. Bloodied but unbroken, Terwilliger was dragged to the pit. The journey was a blur of pain, his body registering every rough handling, every careless impact with the walls as they descended deeper into the warren's forgotten levels.

He was dropped unceremoniously into the pit – a narrow shaft with slick walls that offered no purchase for climbing, water seeping in at ankle height. No light penetrated this deep, leaving prisoners in perpetual darkness, with only their own thoughts for company. It was solitude weaponised, despair made tangible.

As the guards secured the heavy cover over the opening, blocking out the last glimmer of torchlight, Terwilliger allowed himself to sag against the wall. The cold surface against his back offered minimal relief for his abused body. He had survived the questioning, had revealed nothing of value. But he was trapped, removed from the resistance at a critical moment. Victory and defeat had become indistinguishable, tangled in a knot of pain he lacked the strength to unravel.

"Not the outcome we hoped for," Silia's voice came from the darkness, her spectral glow providing the faintest illumination, a ghostly blue that defined the confines of his prison with merciless clarity. "But not the end either."

"How can you say that?" Terwilliger's voice was raw from screaming, barely more than a hoarse whisper in the dank air. "I've failed before we even began. The others will scatter now, too frightened to continue. Everything we've worked for, gone in a single night."

"You underestimate the power of martyrdom," Silia replied. "News of your defiance is already spreading through the burrow. Tansy's network made sure of it. Your capture has done what slow, cautious recruitment could not – it has made the resistance real in the minds of those who were too afraid to act."

"Wonderful. They can tell stories about me after I starve to death in this hole." Bitterness seeped into Terwilliger's tone, the cold water numbing his paws, threatening hypothermia if starvation didn't claim him first.

"Or," Silia countered, her spectral form growing brighter as if fuelled by her conviction, "they can orchestrate a rescue before that happens. Your capture was a setback, not an end. The others will regroup – they have Sage's wisdom, Briarwood's strength, Reed's tactical knowledge. They won't abandon you or the cause."

Terwilliger laughed bitterly, the sound echoing hollowly in the confined space. "The pit is inescapable. That's its purpose. Thornback designed it that way – a slow death with plenty of time to regret defiance."

"From the inside, yes. But what about from the outside?" The ghostly mouse circled the tiny space, examining the wall with speculative interest, her translucent paws passing through it as she assessed the structure. "These lower levels were dug by the earliest inhabitants of Woodburrow, before modern reinforcement techniques. The walls between chambers are thinner than you might expect, especially near water sources."

A tiny spark of hope flickered in Terwilliger's chest, fragile as the first green shoot after winter. "You think they could dig through?"

"With the right knowledge and tools? Absolutely." Silia's confident tone bolstered his failing courage. "The resistance includes burrowers with generations of tunnel-crafting in their bloodlines. And Sage – Sage knows these depths better than Thornback ever will." She moved closer, her presence creating a pocket of cooler air near his face. "Rest now. Conserve your strength. Help will come – but you must be ready when it does."

Despite the cold water numbing his paws and the pain radiating from his torture wounds, Terwilliger managed to find a position that allowed for fitful sleep. His dreams were chaotic – visions of battle, of freedom, of failure; of Thornback's mocking laughter and endless tunnels that led nowhere. But throughout them all ran a constant thread: Silia's voice, guiding, encouraging, demanding that he survive. Not just for himself, but for all of Woodburrow.

***

Terwilliger awakened to the sound of scratching – faint at first, then growing more distinct. It was coming from the wall to his right, accompanied by muffled voices too low to distinguish words but carrying the unmistakable cadence of purposeful work. The sound penetrated the fog of pain and exhaustion that had enveloped him during his imprisonment.

"They're here," Silia announced, her spectral form moving rapidly between Terwilliger and the source of the sound. "Just as I predicted. Your friends have not abandoned you, Terwilliger. They have come."

The scratching continued for what felt like hours before a small shower of dirt preceded the appearance of a hole no larger than Terwilliger's paw. A beam of light – blindingly bright after his time in darkness – pierced through, accompanied by a whispered voice that carried the sweetness of salvation.

"Terwilliger? Are you alive?" The rough concern in the voice was unmistakably Briarwood's.

"Barely," he rasped back. "But functional."

"Stand back. We're widening the hole. It's going to get dusty." The instruction was followed by intensified scratching and the sound of multiple diggers working in co-ordinated shifts.

More digging followed, accompanied by occasional whispered consultations and the shuffling sounds of workers rotating positions. The opening gradually expanded until it was just large enough for a rabbit to squeeze through – a tight fit that would require contortion, but possible. A rope of braided vines was passed through, followed by a small waterskin and a bundle of herbs wrapped in a leaf packet.

"Medicine first," Briarwood instructed, her no-nonsense tone brooking no argument. "Then we'll extract you. We don't have much time. Use the poultice on your worst injuries, drink all the water. You'll need your strength."

The herbal poultice burned as Terwilliger applied it to his wounds, the mixture of crushed leaves and root paste sending fire through his nerves before blessed numbness followed. The water tasted sweeter than anything he could remember, washing away the metallic tang of blood that had lingered in his mouth for hours.

"Ready," he finally said, securing the vine rope around his midsection with paws that felt clumsy and distant. The bindings his captors had used had left deep abrasions.

With slow, careful movements, he eased himself into the tunnel his rescuers had created. It was a tight fit, the rough wall scraping against his injuries, but the promise of freedom propelled him forward. Inch by painful inch, he wormed through the narrow passage, following the gentle but insistent tugging on the vine rope secured around him.

Briarwood and Reed pulled steadily on the rope, helping Terwilliger navigate the cramped passage. After what seemed like an eternity of claustrophobic struggle, he emerged into a small maintenance tunnel where a group of five rabbits waited. Their faces, illuminated by dim lamplight, showed a mixture of relief and shock at his condition.

"We need to move quickly," Reed urged, supporting Terwilliger as he struggled to stand on legs weakened by confinement and injury. The former guard's eyes continually scanned the tunnel in both directions, alert for danger. "The next guard patrol passes the upper junction soon. If they notice anything amiss at the pit…"

"Where are we going?" Terwilliger asked, his voice barely above a whisper, each word an effort that seemed to drain what little strength remained. "The entire burrow will be looking for me. There's nowhere to hide." Despair threatened to overwhelm the brief surge of hope his rescue had kindled.

"Not the entire burrow," Briarwood responded with a grim smile that held more determination than humour. "Just Thornback's loyalists. And they'll be searching all the wrong places." She exchanged a meaningful glance with Reed. "We've been busy while you entertained the Sovereign's hospitality."

They helped Terwilliger through a series of narrow, seldom-used tunnels that descended deeper than he had ever ventured. The passages twisted and turned, sometimes requiring them to crawl on bellies through spaces barely large enough to accommodate them. The air grew noticeably damper, with fungal growths casting a faint bioluminescence on the walls. Strange formations of stone hung from ceilings, built up by centuries of mineral-laden water dripping from above. Eventually, the passage opened into a chamber that momentarily stole Terwilliger's breath, despite his weakened state.

It was vast – far larger than the Gathering Roots – with a ceiling so high it disappeared into shadow. Stone columns, shaped by the slow accumulation of mineral deposits, created natural divisions throughout the space. Most surprisingly, the chamber was occupied. Dozens of rabbits moved about purposefully, speaking in hushed but determined tones. The space hummed with activity, but it was controlled, disciplined – not the chaos of refugees but the ordered intent of community.

"Welcome," Sage said, emerging from behind one of the columns, his elderly frame seeming revitalised in this ancient place, "to Old Warren." The elder's eyes shone with pride as he gestured to the bustling chamber.

Terwilliger stared in disbelief, his pain momentarily forgotten in wonder. "I never knew this existed." The scale of the place, the organised activity, the sense of purpose that pervaded the space – all represented a resistance far beyond what he had imagined possible.

"Few do," the elderly rabbit replied, leading them deeper into the chamber where a makeshift medical area had been established. "Thornback ordered these lower chambers to be sealed years ago, claiming they were structurally unsound. In truth, he feared them because they represented history he couldn't control – proof that the burrow existed long before him and would continue long after." Sage's voice took on the cadence of a historian recounting sacred texts. "These chambers are mentioned in our oldest stories – the founding place where our ancestors first established Woodburrow."

"We've been preparing this place as a refuge," Tansy explained, approaching with fresh bandages and medicine more sophisticated than the emergency poultice applied earlier. Her face was drawn with concern as she assessed Terwilliger's injuries. "After your capture, the plan accelerated. Nearly sixty rabbits have joined us now, with more arriving each day. Your defiance inspired many who had been hesitant."

As Tansy treated his wounds with gentle efficiency, Terwilliger absorbed the implications of what he was seeing. This wasn't just a hiding place – it was becoming an alternative community, a shadow burrow growing beneath the tyrant's very paws. Rabbits of all ages moved with purpose: youngsters carrying messages, adults organising supplies, elders teaching skills long forgotten under Thornback's regime.

Silia floated nearby, her spectral eyes shining with satisfaction. "I told you your capture would galvanise them," she murmured, her form more vibrant than Terwilliger had ever seen it. "Sometimes, apparent defeat is merely a prelude to greater victory. Your suffering was not in vain."

But despite the impressive organisation before him, doubt gnawed at Terwilliger. The weight of responsibility settled heavily on shoulders already burdened by physical pain. "Sixty rabbits is barely a tenth of Woodburrow's population," he noted, keeping his voice low so only those directly around him could hear. "And we're still outnumbered by Thornback's guards. He controls the food, the water sources. How long can we survive down here, cut off from the rest of the burrow?"

"Numbers aren't everything," Reed countered, his military experience evident in his assessment. "We have surprise, determination, and increasingly, we have the moral authority. Each new cruelty Thornback inflicts drives more to our cause. Guards who once were loyal begin to question when ordered to punish their own kin."

"And," Briarwood added with uncharacteristic gentleness, her usually gruff demeanour softened by something like respect, "we have you – living proof that one can defy Thornback and survive. His power rests on fear, on the belief that resistance is futile. You've shattered that belief."

The burden of their expectations settled heavily on Terwilliger. These rabbits had risked everything to rescue him, believing he represented hope for a better future. The responsibility was terrifying, especially in his weakened state. Could he live up to their faith? Did he even have a choice?

"I need time to recover," he said finally, acknowledging both his physical limitations and his need to process everything that had happened. "And then we'll plan our next move."

Sage nodded approvingly. "Wise, Terwilliger. Rest now. Tomorrow will bring challenges enough."

As the others dispersed to their various duties, Terwilliger found himself alone with Silia in a small alcove that had been prepared for him. Fresh bedding of dried moss, carefully arranged and unexpectedly plush, offered more comfort than he was used to.

"You're angry with me," Silia observed, her translucent form hovering at the edge of the alcove.

"You knew this would happen," Terwilliger accused, his voice low to avoid being overheard. His fur still bore the matted evidence of his ordeal, and every movement sent ripples of pain through his battered body. "You knew I'd be captured, tortured."

The ghostly mouse didn't deny it. Her ethereal features remained composed, almost serene in their translucency. "I knew it was possible. Just as I knew it might be necessary." There was no apology in her voice, only a calm certainty that somehow made her admission more infuriating.

"Necessary?!" Terwilliger nearly shouted before catching himself, glancing anxiously towards the alcove entrance. The last thing the resistance needed was to see him arguing with thin air. He lowered his voice to a harsh whisper. "How was my suffering necessary?"

"Revolutions require symbols, Terwilliger. Martyrs, preferably living ones." Silia's voice was gentle but unapologetic. "Your defiance of Thornback, your refusal to break under questioning – these acts have transformed you from a solitary malcontent into a leader worth following." She drifted closer, her ghostly eyes reflecting centuries of similar struggles. "The others speak of you in whispers of awe now."

"You manipulated me. Used me as a pawn in your game." Terwilliger's ears flattened against his head, his injuries throbbing in rhythm with his accelerated heartbeat.

"Not a pawn," Silia corrected, a hint of sharpness entering her ethereal voice. "A knight, perhaps. Or a rook. Valuable, powerful, essential to victory." She moved closer still, her presence causing the temperature around him to drop noticeably. The chill penetrated his fur, making his wounds ache more intensely. "And this is no game. The future of Woodburrow – of all who dwell within it – hangs in the balance. Every kit born into freedom instead of fear justifies your path."

Terwilliger turned away, the moss bedding rustling beneath him as he shifted his weight to ease the pressure from some of his injuries.

He was too exhausted and pained to continue the argument, his body demanding respite despite the turmoil in his mind. "Leave me. I need to sleep." His voice cracked slightly, betraying the depth of his physical and emotional exhaustion.

Silia obeyed without further comment, her ghostly form fading from view. The alcove seemed to warm immediately in her absence, though the chill of her revelations lingered in Terwilliger's thoughts.

Chapter Six

Sleep, when it came, brought nightmares of the questioning chamber, of darkness and drowning in the pit. The sensation of water filling his lungs felt horrifyingly real, causing Terwilliger to thrash against the moss bedding. He awoke multiple times, gasping and disorientated. Each time, the pain of his injuries dragged him back to a reality that offered little more comfort than his dreams. Finally, he surrendered to restless wakefulness as the burrow's distant rhythms – the subtle changes in airflow, the altered patterns of movement from the levels above – suggested morning had arrived.

To his surprise, Silia was nowhere to be seen. Since their first encounter at the northern exit, she had rarely left his side for more than brief periods, her spectral presence a constant companion whether welcome or not. Her absence now felt strangely disquieting, despite his anger towards her. The alcove seemed larger without her, emptier somehow.

Rising painfully, each movement requiring deliberate care to avoid reopening wounds, Terwilliger made his way from his alcove into the main chamber of Old Warren. The expansive space, carved from the earth centuries before, buzzed with purposeful activity, giving the impression of a fully functioning community rather than a band of fugitives. Rabbits moved with determination between workstations, their voices a low murmur.

Briarwood spotted Terwilliger from across the chamber and approached with brisk efficiency, a wooden cup in her paw. Steam rose from the dark liquid within, carrying a bitter, medicinal aroma. "Willow bark tea," she explained, offering it to him with detached, matter-of-fact concern. "For the pain. I've added a touch of honey from our emergency stores." Her practical demeanour couldn't quite mask the sympathetic wince as she observed his laboured movements.

Terwilliger accepted gratefully, the warmth of the cup seeping into his paws as he inhaled the astringent steam. The first sip was bitter despite the honey, but he welcomed it, knowing the relief it would eventually bring. "Any news from above?" he asked, his voice still rough from sleep and lingering trauma.

"Thornback has gone into a rage over your escape. Doubled the guard, instituted a burrow-wide curfew." Her whiskers twitched in grim amusement, the slight motion revealing more satisfaction than her controlled expression allowed. "He's also ordered the questioning of anyone known to associate with you, which has mainly resulted in more recruits for our cause as friends and family flee to avoid his wrath. His heavy-handedness does our recruitment for us."

"So we grow stronger while he weakens himself," Terwilliger mused, taking another sip of the medicinal tea. Already he could feel the edge of his pain beginning to dull, allowing him to stand a little straighter.

"Precisely." Briarwood gestured towards a large flat stone where maps and plans were spread out, weighted down with pebbles and small carved markers. The stone table stood in the centre of the chamber, clearly the headquarters of their operation. "We've been developing a strategy while you recovered. Would you care to review it? Your perspective would be valuable."

For the next several hours, Terwilliger immersed himself in the resistance's plans, the willow bark tea gradually easing his physical discomfort as he focused on the task at hand. They had been busy during his captivity – mapping guard rotations with meticulous attention to detail, identifying sympathisers within Thornback's inner circle through carefully cultivated contacts, stockpiling weapons and supplies in hidden caches throughout the lower tunnels. The level of organisation impressed him, though he noted several tactical weaknesses that his unique perspective could help address.

Around him, the bustling activity of Old Warren continued unabated – rabbits training with improvised weapons in one corner, others preparing meals from carefully rationed supplies. The atmosphere held a strange mixture of tension and hope, fear and determination.

It was late afternoon when Silia finally reappeared, materialising beside Terwilliger as he studied a diagram of the burrow's main ventilation shafts. Her sudden presence sent a chill through the air that made him shudder, though a part of him was relieved to see her.

"I've been scouting," she announced without preamble, her ghostly form more agitated than usual. "Thornback is planning something significant. The guards are gathering weapons, preparing for what appears to be a major action." Her words fell like stones into the quiet concentration that had surrounded Terwilliger's planning session.

"Against us?" Terwilliger asked, their earlier argument temporarily forgotten in the face of this new threat. He straightened, ignoring the protest of his injuries, his full attention on the spectral mouse.

"I believe so. Someone must have reported unusual activity near the sealed entrances to these lower chambers." Silia's spectral tail lashed with unease, passing through a nearby stack of supplies without disturbing them.

"They're methodically searching the old tunnels, section by section. It's only a matter of time before they discover this place. I watched them break through a wall I thought was impenetrable."

Terwilliger felt his heart sink. Just when they had established a secure base, just when their numbers were growing and their plans developing, they faced discovery and potential annihilation. The faces of every rabbit who had joined their cause flashed through his mind – all counting on him, all at risk.

"We need to evacuate," he began, already mentally cataloguing possible escape routes.

Silia shook her head. "It's too late for that. The connecting tunnels are already being patrolled. And where would at least sixty rabbits go without being noticed?" Her ghostly voice hardened. "Thornback's guards are checking every passage, every crevice. Moving now would mean certain capture."

"Then what do you suggest? We can't simply wait to be found." Terwilliger's voice remained steady despite the panic threatening to rise within him. Around them, several resistance members had noticed his intense conversation with what appeared to be empty air, but they had grown accustomed to his apparent soliloquies.

The ghostly mouse's eyes gleamed with an ancient warrior's calculation, centuries of conflict reflected in her spectral gaze. "We strike first." The words hung in the air, bold and dangerous.

"Strike first?!" Terwilliger echoed, studying Silia's expression, searching for any sign of doubt and finding none. "We're outnumbered, outarmed, and many of us are simply too weak." He gestured to his own battered body as evidence. "A direct confrontation seems reckless at best."

Silia floated closer, her ethereal form pulsing with an intensity that stirred the air around Terwilliger like a breeze. "Conventional warfare would indeed be suicide. But we have advantages Thornback cannot anticipate." She gestured around the vast chamber of Old Warren, her spectral paw sweeping to encompass the ancient architecture. "Knowledge of these ancient passages that even Thornback's oldest advisors have forgotten. The element of surprise. And..." her ghostly eyes locked with his, intense and unwavering, "...a leader who has already proven impossible to break."

Terwilliger still didn't see himself as a leader. He didn't crave command or carry the certainty that others seemed to expect. But with each passing hour, as the odds tilted further against them, it became clear that choice had little to do with it. A plan began to form in his mind – audacious, perhaps even foolhardy, but with a slim chance of success. The pain of his injuries receded as his thoughts raced ahead, examining possibilities and consequences with newfound clarity. He called the resistance together, including Reed with his guard experience and several of the burrow's most knowledgeable tunnellers.

"Thornback's power relies on three things," he began as others gathered close, ears forward in intense concentration. "His personal guard, his control of food supplies, and the fear he instils in the general population. We need to neutralise all three simultaneously." As he spoke, his voice grew stronger, more assured, the mantle of leadership settling on his shoulders with unexpected naturalness.

Over the next hour, a daring strategy emerged, refined by input from all present. The resistance would divide into three teams, each with a specific objective. Briarwood would lead an assault on the food storage chambers, securing and redistributing supplies to demonstrate Thornback's vulnerability and win popular support. Reed would co-ordinate a diversionary attack to draw the majority of guards away from the central chambers, using his knowledge of guard protocols to maximum effect. And Terwilliger, secretly guided by Silia's ancient wisdom, would lead a small strike force directly against Thornback himself.

The plan took shape – timing co-ordinated, contingencies considered. Questions were raised and addressed, weak points identified and reinforced. Throughout the discussion, Terwilliger found himself glancing at Silia several times, her ghostly presence hovering beside him, offering whispered suggestions that only he could hear.

"The timing must be perfect," Terwilliger emphasised. "If any element fails, the entire plan collapses. We'll have only one chance at this."

"Dawn tomorrow," Briarwood suggested, her practical nature asserting itself. Her eyes, sharp and calculating, scanned the assembled rabbits. "Most of the guards will be tired from night patrol, and the burrow will be stirring – potential allies everywhere. The changing of the watch always creates distractions we can exploit."

***

As preparations continued through the night – weapons distributed, teams organised, final instructions given – the chamber of Old Warren pulsed with nervous energy. Every rabbit understood the stakes, knew that by morning they would either be victorious or defeated, perhaps dead. Yet there was surprisingly little fear evident in their movements, only determination and a fierce, quiet resolve.

Terwilliger found a quiet moment to speak privately with Silia, retreating to a small side tunnel away from the bustling activity. "If we fail tomorrow," he said softly, the weight of responsibility evident in every syllable, "many will die. Perhaps all who've followed me." He traced a pattern in the dirt, not meeting the ghost's gaze. "Their blood will be on my paws."

"Any resistance against tyranny carries such risks. None of them joined your cause without understanding the potential cost," she said gently. "But remember why you chose to stay that night at the northern exit, Terwilliger. Not just to oppose Thornback, but to fight for a better Woodburrow. For a community where rabbits live by the old values – co-operation over coercion, wisdom over force."

"I'm still angry at myself for letting you persuade me to stay," he admitted, meeting her spectral gaze directly for the first time since their argument.

"As you should be," she replied with surprising candour, no defensiveness in her ethereal tone. "I pushed you into a role you didn't seek, knowing the cost would be high. I witnessed your suffering with no small measure of guilt." Her spectral paw reached towards him, passing through his fur with a chill that raised goosebumps beneath his coat. "But I did so believing you were Woodburrow's best hope. I still believe that."

Terwilliger sighed, observing the busy preparations close by – rabbits checking improvised weapons, whispering final instructions, some pausing to share meaningful embraces that might be their last. "Let's hope your faith isn't misplaced." He winced as his injuries protested, then squared his shoulders and returned to the main chamber.

Chapter Seven

Dawn approached with the certainty of the seasons. The resistance fighters made final adjustments to their weapons – crude but effective spears, slings, and daggers crafted from materials scavenged. The weapons bore the marks of hasty creation, yet each had been tested and honed to lethal sharpness, balanced for the paws that would wield them. Small groups gathered in tight circles to share quiet words of encouragement or to whisper ancient prayers for protection, their breath forming small clouds in the cool underground air.

Terwilliger moved among them with measured steps, ignoring the persistent ache of his healing wounds. He offered steady reassurance despite the doubts churning within him. The weight of their trust pressed heavier upon his shoulders than any physical burden he had ever carried. His own strike team consisted of six agile rabbits who could move swiftly and silently through the narrow maintenance tunnels that would provide their approach to Thornback's chamber. Each had been selected not only for their physical prowess but for the unwavering determination that burned in their eyes.

As the first distant sounds of activity filtered down from the upper burrow – the shuffle of countless paws on packed earth, the murmur of voices rising and falling – indicating the dawn gathering was beginning, Terwilliger gave the signal with a curt nod. The three teams moved out through separate exits, their forms quickly swallowed by shadow as each followed carefully memorised routes that would keep them hidden until the crucial moment. The fate of Woodburrow rested on their synchronicity, on each rabbit performing their role without hesitation or error.

Terwilliger's path took them through the oldest sections of Woodburrow, tunnels so ancient that roots from long-dead trees still formed part of their structure, twisted and petrified into strange, reaching shapes. The air tasted of earth and time, carrying whispers of generations past. Silia led the way, her ghostly glow visible only to Terwilliger, casting a blue-white light that made the world feel suspended between reality and dream.

"Thornback's chamber lies directly above us now," she said as they reached a vertical shaft reinforced with ancient wooden supports, weathered and grey with age. Her voice, though quiet, seemed to reverberate through the abandoned passage. "This ventilation tunnel hasn't been used in generations. It will bring us out behind Thornback's platform." Her spectral form pulsed faintly with anticipation – the only sign of her anxiety in this critical moment.

One by one, the strike team ascended the narrow shaft, careful not to dislodge the fragile supports that creaked and groaned under even their lightest touch. Each fighter moved with determined silence, communicating only through gestures and meaningful glances. Terwilliger went last, his still-healing injuries protesting with every movement, sending sharp jabs of pain through his side and shoulder.

Near the top, he paused to listen, ears swivelling to catch every nuance of sound: the muffled patter of hundreds of rabbits gathered above, the restless shifting of bodies, the occasional cough or whispered exchange – and one voice rising above it all: Thornback's, addressing the crowd with the practiced cadence of authority.

"...cannot tolerate dissent that threatens our very survival," the tyrant was saying, his voice carrying the confidence of one accustomed to unquestioning obedience. The deep timbre resonated through the wooden platform above, vibrating the very air around Terwilliger. "The escaped prisoner and his accomplices represent a dangerous element that must be eliminated for the continued prosperity of our burrow."

Silia floated back down the shaft, her form passing through the wooden supports as though they were merely smoke. "Reed's diversion will begin any moment," she whispered, her voice carrying no further than Terwilliger's ears. "When you hear it, that's our signal."

Terwilliger nodded, readying himself for

what was to come. His dagger – a replacement for the one confiscated during his capture – was secured at his waist. It didn't yet feel familiar in his grip, but its presence was a small comfort nonetheless.

A distant commotion rippled through the chamber, followed by shouts of alarm from the rear. The sound swelled like a wave, confusion spreading through the gathered crowd. Reed's attack had begun, right on schedule. Terwilliger felt a surge of fierce pride in his comrades' discipline and courage.

"Now!" Silia urged, her spectral form brightening with urgency.

Terwilliger and his team burst from the ventilation shaft in a shower of ancient dust and debris, tiny splinters and dirt raining down as they emerged directly behind the raised platform where Thornback stood. The tyrant spun around with surprising agility for his size, eyes widening in shock as he recognised the rabbit leading the assault.

"You!" he snarled, his upper lip curling to reveal yellowed incisors. He reached for the ceremonial spear that was more symbol than weapon, its shaft polished to a high shine.

But Terwilliger was already in motion, muscles bunching and releasing as he leapt onto the platform with a speed born of desperation. The guards flanking Thornback – burly rabbits with hard eyes and harder hearts – moved to intercept, only to be engaged by the rest of the strike team in a flurry of calculated violence.

"Rabbits of Woodburrow!" Terwilliger shouted, his voice carrying over the growing chaos, ringing off the walls of the chamber. "The time has come to reclaim our burrow!"

Throughout the massive chamber, tension snapped into open conflict as resistance members who had infiltrated the gathering revealed themselves, pulling hidden weapons from beneath clothing. The confused masses of ordinary rabbits pressed back against the walls, ears flat against their heads, uncertain which side to support, their eyes wide with fear and growing understanding.

Thornback, momentarily separated from his guards by the swift assault, faced Terwilliger alone on the central portion of the platform. The larger rabbit's size and strength were formidable, his well-fed bulk and muscled limbs making him a daunting opponent, but Terwilliger had the advantages of speed and righteous fury burning in his veins like fire.

"You're a fool," Thornback growled, circling warily. His breath came in controlled measures, betraying his own combat experience. "Even if you kill me, another will take my place. Order must be maintained."

"Not your kind of order," Terwilliger replied, matching the tyrant's movements step for step, his body held loose and ready. "Woodburrow thrived for generations before your reign of terror. It will thrive again once you're removed."

With a roar that seemed to shake dust from the ceiling, Thornback charged, bringing his ceremonial spear to bear with surprising speed. The weapon's ornate head flashed in the filtered light. Terwilliger sidestepped, his smaller stature allowing him to pivot on a single paw, scoring a shallow cut along the larger rabbit's flank with his dagger. Blood welled immediately, staining the tyrant's pristine fur. Enraged, Thornback swung again with renewed ferocity, this time catching Terwilliger across the shoulder, reopening one of his torture wounds with a tearing sound that was nearly drowned out by the clamour of battle surrounding them.

Pain lanced through Terwilliger's body like liquid fire, nearly causing him to drop his weapon as his vision momentarily swam with bright spots. The metallic scent of his own blood filled his nostrils, triggering recent memories of the questioning chamber.

"Steady," Silia's voice came from beside him, inaudible to anyone else, cool and calming like water over heated stone. "He's stronger but slower. Use that."

Forcing himself to focus through the pain, calling upon reserves of strength he had carefully cultivated for this moment, Terwilliger feinted left, watching as Thornback's weight shifted to compensate, then darted right as the tyrant lunged with predictable force. The tyrant's momentum carried him forward, off-balance for a crucial half-second, and Terwilliger struck – a quick, precise jab that embedded his dagger in

Thornback's hindquarter, slicing through muscle with sickening resistance.

The larger rabbit howled in pain and fury, a sound more beast than rabbit, spinning with unexpected speed to backhand Terwilliger across the face with a paw like a sledgehammer. The blow connected with bone-jarring force, sending him sprawling to the edge of the platform, momentarily stunned as stars exploded behind his eyes and the taste of copper flooded his mouth.

Thornback advanced, limping but deadly, each step leaving a small smear of blood on the platform, spear raised for a killing thrust. His shadow fell across Terwilliger's prone form like a shroud. "You should have surrendered when you had the chance," he snarled through gritted teeth, his voice thick with hatred.

As the spear descended in a whistling arc, Terwilliger rolled aside with millimetres to spare, the weapon splintering against the platform with a crack like breaking bones. In the same fluid motion, he swept Thornback's legs from under him, exploiting the tyrant's weakened stance, sending the wounded rabbit crashing down.

They grappled fiercely, rolling across the platform as the battle raged around them – a cacophony of shouts, cries, and the clatter of improvised weapons. Terwilliger caught glimpses of the wider conflict: Reed's fighters pressing their advantage, ordinary rabbits beginning to choose sides – but his world narrowed to this desperate struggle. Thornback's greater weight threatened to crush him, massive paws searching for vulnerable points, but Terwilliger, despite his smaller size, fought with the accumulated rage of years of oppression, every dirty trick and desperate move he had ever learnt coming into play.

"You fight well for a runt," Thornback growled, blood from his wounds matting his once-sleek fur into dark, sticky clumps. His breath came in ragged gasps, hot against Terwilliger's face. "But you can't win. My guards will slaughter your pathetic rebellion like newborn kits."

"Look around you," Terwilliger countered, struggling to break the larger rabbit's grip on his throat, feeling his windpipe begin to compress under the relentless pressure. Black spots danced at the edges of his vision.

"Your guards are falling. The rabbits you terrorised are finding their courage."

Indeed, throughout the chamber, the tide was turning. Reed's fighters had neutralised many of the guards. More importantly, ordinary rabbits, inspired by the resistance's bold action, were beginning to join the fight against their oppressors, grabbing fallen weapons or using whatever came to paw.

Thornback's grip tightened, digging into fur and flesh, cutting off Terwilliger's air with implacable force. "Then I'll at least have the satisfaction of killing you before I fall."

Darkness crept into the edges of Terwilliger's vision as he fought desperately for breath, his lungs burning for air that wouldn't come. His paws scrabbled uselessly against Thornback's arms, seeking any leverage, any weakness in the vice-like grip. The sounds of battle seemed to recede, as though heard from underwater.

"Reach for that abandoned dagger on your right!" Silia urged, her spectral form circling the struggling pair like an agitated firefly, her voice cutting through Terwilliger's fading consciousness.

With his last reserves of strength, muscles screaming in protest, Terwilliger cast a desperate glance towards the edge of the platform. There, partially obscured by the shifting chaos of battle, a dagger lay discarded, presumably dropped by a rabbit in the fray. It was just within reach, its blade gleaming with promise.

With a final surge of determination, Terwilliger stretched out, his paw groping for the vital lifeline. In one swift motion, driven by survival instinct and the last sparks of his fading consciousness, he seized the weapon and plunged it into Thornback's side, overwhelmed by the sensation of parting flesh.

Thornback's eyes widened in shock and pain, his pupils contracting to pinpoints. His grip loosened as a shudder ran through his massive frame, allowing Terwilliger to heave him aside with strength born of pure desperation and scramble to his feet, gasping for air. Each breath was agony through his bruised throat, the sweet rush of oxygen almost painful as it filled his deprived lungs.

The wounded tyrant struggled to rise, one paw pressed against his bleeding side, crimson seeping beyond the feeble tourniquet – a physical manifestation of his crumbling authority. "Finish it then," he growled, defiant even in defeat. "Prove you're no better than me."

Terwilliger stood over his fallen opponent, dagger raised and slick with blood. His arm trembled not with weakness but with the enormity of the decision before him. The chamber had grown strangely quiet, the sounds of combat fading as hundreds of eyes turned towards the confrontation at its centre. This moment, Terwilliger realised with clarity, would define everything that followed. It would set the course for Woodburrow's future as surely as any proclamation or decree.

"No," he said finally, his voice rough from Thornback's strangling grip but carrying clearly in the hushed chamber. He lowered the weapon deliberately, making sure every rabbit watching could see his choice. "Your fate will be decided by those you've wronged, not by me alone."

Briarwood's voice rang out from across the chamber, breathless but triumphant: "The storage chambers are open! From now on, every rabbit eats their fill – food will be shared equally across all sections!"

A cheer rose from the gathered rabbits, tentative at first, then growing in volume like a summer storm as the implications became clear. Thornback's power was broken, his carefully constructed system of inequality dismantled.

As guards loyal to the tyrant laid down their weapons one by one, surrendering to the inevitable with varying degrees of reluctance, Terwilliger addressed the assembled burrow.

"For too long, we've lived in fear," he announced, his voice still weak but strengthening with each word. "For too long, we've accepted cruelty as the price of survival." His gaze swept the chamber, connecting with as many eyes as possible – young and old, supporters and former opponents alike. "No more. Today, we reclaim Woodburrow for all who dwell within it."

The response was thunderous – a release of long-suppressed hope and determination that echoed through the chamber, rattling dirt from the ceiling and causing the roots overhead to tremble as though the very trees above were awakening to a new age. Rabbits embraced, some weeping openly, others standing in stunned silence as the reality of their liberation sank in.

Silia floated beside Terwilliger, her spectral face alight with satisfaction. "Well done," she whispered, her voice carrying notes of both pride and caution. "The hard part begins now."

Looking out over the cheering crowd, at the wounded being attended to by impromptu medics, at former enemies cautiously beginning to communicate across divisions that had seemed insurmountable only hours before, Terwilliger knew she was right. His body ached from many injuries old and new, but his mind was already racing ahead to the challenges that awaited. Winning freedom was only the first step, a beginning rather than an end. Building a just society, healing the wounds of division, establishing systems that would prevent another Thornback from rising – these would be the true challenges.

But for this moment – this bright, blood-earned moment suspended between what was and what might be – it was enough to know that the long night of Thornback's reign had finally ended. Dawn had truly come to Woodburrow at last, and with it, the promise of renewal.

Chapter Eight

Weeks later, as Terwilliger reclined on his bed of fresh moss and sweet-smelling grasses, change had settled like spring rain. The jagged wound Thornback had reopened during their desperate battle still throbbed persistently with the memory of violence, but like the burrow itself, it was healing remarkably well.

"You should have Tansy look at that again," Silia advised. "She has quite the gift for healing herbs, that one."

Terwilliger smiled warmly at the ghostly mouse. "I have – this morning, before the council meeting. She says I'm healing faster than expected – like everyone else in Woodburrow."

It was undeniably true. Throughout every corner and chamber of Woodburrow, rabbits were recovering from their wounds – both physical and spiritual – at an astonishing rate. Without the constant, gnawing stress of Thornback's reign of terror, without the perpetual hunger of insufficient rations and the bone-deep exhaustion of forced labour, bodies were finally able to heal as nature intended. The food stores, now managed efficiently by a rotating committee and distributed equally according to need rather than status, ensured that everyone from elders to kits had enough nourishment to thrive.

Thornback himself, despite his countless cruelties, had been treated with a dignity and compassion he had never shown to others during his blood-soaked rule. Despite passionate calls from some quarters for retribution – particularly from those who bore permanent torture scars – the newly formed council had insisted on nursing the fallen tyrant back to health with the same care given to all wounded rabbits. Their unexpected mercy, however, came with one non-negotiable condition: upon recovery, he would leave Woodburrow forever, banished from the community he had so brutally dominated. Ironically, in a final act of defiance, Thornback hadn't waited for his full healing. Still visibly limping from his wounds and with fur stained with seeping blood, he had departed the burrow under cover of pre-dawn darkness. Pride, it seemed, was a more powerful driving force than physical pain – he couldn't bear to face as equals those he had once commanded with absolute authority.

A dozen of his most fanatical followers – those whose cruelty had matched or even surpassed their master's – had gone with him, unwilling or perhaps fundamentally unable to imagine life in a changed Woodburrow where their former victims now stood as their equals. The rest of his former guards, however, had surprised everyone with their almost desperate eagerness to integrate into the new society, as if relieved to shed the heavy mantle of oppressor. Reed had been instrumental in bringing them into the new security rotation, where they now served as protectors rather than enforcers, their knowledge of defensive tactics proving invaluable. As it turned out, many had been acting from fear rather than genuine conviction all along, their loyalty purchased with threats rather than freely given.

Terwilliger finally broke the peaceful silence, his voice slightly rough with emotion. "I owe you an apology, Silia. A profound one."

The spectral mouse tilted her head. "For what, precisely?"

"For doubting you. For the bitter anger I directed at you after my capture."

Silia's ethereal form drifted closer, the temperature around Terwilliger dropping noticeably. "Your anger was entirely justified, Terwilliger. I pushed you towards tremendous danger, knowing full well the risks you faced."

"But you were right," Terwilliger insisted, sitting up straighter, his ears perking forward with conviction. "If I had fled that night as I planned, if I had abandoned Woodburrow to save my own pelt..." He gestured outwards at the burrow that was transforming daily into something better than it had ever been, even in the oldest memories held by the eldest rabbits. "None of this would have happened. Not one bit of it. And I would have been alone out there in the unforgiving wild, probably dead by now, my body feeding the foxes and crows."

"And in your final moments, you would have been taunted by what could have been if only you had stayed," Silia agreed.

"And more than that," Terwilliger said firmly, "you saved my life. And before that, far more importantly, you saved my soul by making me confront what truly mattered, by refusing to let me take the easy, immediate path of escape." His voice grew softer, weighted with genuine emotion. "Thank you for believing in me when I couldn't find the strength to believe in myself."

Silia's ghostly features softened with pride and affection. "My faith in you never wavered for a single moment, Terwilliger. Not even in your darkest moments of doubt and despair. I would make precisely the same choice again, knowing what has been achieved here through your courage."

Terwilliger nodded slowly, his eyes momentarily distant with memories. "As would I, without hesitation. The torture, the paralysing fear, the crushing uncertainty – it was all worth enduring for what Woodburrow has become." He leaned back against the wall, feeling the cool, packed earth against his fur. "And is still in the process of becoming, day by day."

The innovative council system that had emerged from countless discussions had exceeded everyone's most optimistic expectations. Five representatives chosen democratically, with positions rotating every season to prevent any individual from accumulating too much power or becoming complacent in authority. Significant decisions were made by thoughtful consensus after open discussion where even the youngest and most humble members of the community could speak without fear, ensuring that all voices were heard and respected. There was no sovereign, no single leader who might gradually transform into another Thornback through the subtle corruption of unchecked authority. All rabbits stood as equals, all with a meaningful voice in how precious resources were distributed and necessary labour organised for the common good.

"The council members unanimously wanted me to lead them," Terwilliger said, his ears flicking back in mild embarrassment at the recollection. "I'm glad I respectfully declined the position, despite their persistence."

"You would have surely been an asset to them."

"Perhaps, but I did what was desperately needed when it was needed," Terwilliger explained carefully, his voice steady with quiet conviction. "I'm proud of that, without reservation. But I never wanted to be a leader – certainly not permanently. The very thought fills me with discomfort. I'm much happier now, helping to rebuild alongside others, contributing my paws and ideas as one among many."

"A profoundly wise choice," Silia murmured approvingly. "Power should always be temporary, especially for those clear-sighted enough to understand its subtle dangers and seductions."

They fell silent again, comfortable in each other's presence, the varied sounds of a busy, productive burrow filtering into the chamber from the network of tunnels beyond. A faint shift in the air stirred Terwilliger's fur, though no breeze touched the chamber. Silia's glow, once so vivid in the dark days of rebellion, seemed somehow softer now – calmer, like moonlight fading before the dawn.

"You're leaving soon, aren't you?" Terwilliger said suddenly, the realisation forming in his mind even as he spoke the words aloud.

Silia didn't seem remotely surprised by his perception. "My work here is done," she acknowledged with gentle certainty. "I have accomplished what I came here to do – to witness tyranny overthrown and natural balance restored to this warren."

Terwilliger felt an unexpected tightness constricting his chest, a sense of impending loss he hadn't anticipated. "When will you go?"

"Soon," Silia replied simply, her voice as soft as a distant echo. "Soon."

"Where will you go from here?" Terwilliger asked, struggling to imagine daily life in Woodburrow without her spectral presence.

Silia's translucent form shimmered slightly, rippling like disturbed water. "There are other warrens, other burrows where dangerous imbalance has taken root and injustice flourishes. Or perhaps," she added with uncharacteristic hesitation, "I will finally find peaceful rest – the great mystery that awaits all souls eventually when their earthly purposes are fulfilled." She regarded him with ancient, knowing eyes. "Perhaps I am not destined to forever linger between worlds as I have for so long."

Terwilliger nodded solemnly, accepting her imminent departure though not without profound regret. "I'll miss your invaluable counsel in the days ahead."

"You have all you truly need now – wisdom painstakingly earned through hardship, loyal companions who have proven their unquestionable worth in the crucible of adversity, and a community now united in common purpose." Silia's voice carried absolute certainty, leaving no room for doubt. "My counsel would be entirely redundant in what comes next."

"Not your counsel," Terwilliger corrected gently, his voice warm with genuine feeling. "Your presence. Your friendship. Those can never be replaced."

For a moment, Silia seemed taken aback by his words, then her ghostly features arranged themselves into what might have been a smile of pleasure. "In all my long centuries of watching over the living, precious few have ever called me friend rather than oracle or guide."

"Then they were short-sighted fools," Terwilliger said simply, without hesitation.

"You will do remarkably well, Terwilliger of Woodburrow – you and all who dwell here beneath these protective roots." Her ethereal form began to fade further into invisibility, becoming more translucent with each passing heartbeat. "Remember always that the greatest threat to any community is forgetting what it overcame – and what it sacrificed – to achieve true freedom."

"We won't forget," Terwilliger promised solemnly, rising respectfully to his feet. "I'll personally make certain each new generation understands what was sacrificed by those who came before – and precisely why those sacrifices were necessary."

Silia's form was now barely visible. "Farewell, my dear friend. May your burrow thrive and prosper for a thousand seasons and beyond."

"Farewell, Silia," Terwilliger whispered reverently, watching intently as the last trace of her presence dissolved completely, leaving only memory behind.

For a long, contemplative time after Silia had gone, Terwilliger stood perfectly motionless, feeling both acute loss and profound gratitude in equal measure. Finally, he headed out purposefully, keen to be with the others.

The expansive chamber, once an intimidating setting for Thornback's displays of dominance and arbitrary punishment, had been thoughtfully transformed into a pleasant gathering space for all inhabitants. The raised central platform remained in place but was now respectfully encircled with comfortable seating areas arranged in concentric rings where any rabbit, regardless of age or role, could speak freely and be properly heard by all. Currently, it bustled with enthusiastic activity as extensive preparations for the communal evening meal were well underway.

"There you are at last!" Briarwood called cheerfully, enthusiastically waving Terwilliger over to where a diverse group was intensely studying detailed plans for expanded living quarters sketched on flattened bark. "We were just vigorously debating whether the eastern expansion should prioritise additional individual sleeping chambers for growing families, or expanded communal spaces for gatherings during the coming winter. Your thoughtful perspective would be most valuable."

As Terwilliger readily joined the lively, passionate discussion, offering his considered perspective while carefully ensuring it didn't inadvertently overwhelm other equally valid voices, he felt a profound sense of rightness and belonging settle deep within his heart. This collaborative process, this respectful exchange of differing ideas, was precisely what he had fought and suffered for – not just the blessed absence of tyranny, but the vibrant presence of something immeasurably better.

And somewhere in the deepest, most intuitive part of his being, Terwilliger felt rather than heard Silia's words that he would hold forever as a cherished memory:

No act of compassion is meaningless. The ripples of kindness spread in ways unseen, even in the darkest of times.

As the rejuvenated burrow continued its harmonious collective life around him, Terwilliger knew with unshakable certainty that although challenges would inevitably come with the seasons ahead, Woodburrow's brightest, most glorious days lay ahead rather than behind.

www.ingramcontent.com/pod-product-compliance
Lightning Source LLC
Chambersburg PA
CBHW032018180726

48283CB00008B/2725

9781913779504